Written by JD Green
Illustrated by Jennifer Naalchigar
Designed by Nicola Moore

First published by HOMETOWN WORLD in 2018
Hometown World Ltd
7 Northumberland Buildings
Bath
BA1 2JB

www.hometownworld.co.uk

Follow us @hometownworldbooks

ISBN 978-1-78553-782-0
All rights reserved
Printed in Italy
HTW_PO201809

Ben is so **AMAZING**.

The nicest, smartest guy.

He's **super cool** (and cool kids rule).

It's true! I'll tell you why...

AWESOME!

Ben is very **helpful**.

He gives this mix a beating.

SPLAT!

And when that cake's had time to bake,

he'll help out **with**

the

eating.

Ben is very **caring**.

He's friend to birds and bees,

and **bugs**, and **slugs**, and dogs, and frogs,

and even **cats with fleas!**

PING!

Ben is quite a **rOck star!**

Each time he hears a song,

he sings aloud but does not care

if all the words are wrong!

Ben has such a **lovely** smile

that goes from ear to ear.

Just spending time around him

leaves you feeling full of cheer.

Ben is very **sporting**.
You'll always see him **grinning**.

He won't cry if he **loses**
and he won't boast if he's **winning!**

Not **everything** comes easily.

He practises **a lot!**

And that's how he's developed

the **AMAZING** skills he's got.

Ben is such a **brave** boy.

This spider's **not** a threat!

He picks it up, **gives it a name**

and keeps it as **his pet!**

There's always **fun** and **laughter**
everywhere Ben goes.

He likes to dance around a lot
and strike a funky pose...

COOL!

Ben is very **generous**

with all his awesome toys.

He shares them out when playing with

the other **girls** and **boys**.

THE BEST!

Ben is so **AMAZING**.

What sets this boy apart

is that he's **cool**, and **brave**, and **fun**,

and has a **GREAT**

BIG

HEART!